READ ALL OF FRANNY'S ADVENTURES

Franny K. Stein
MAD SCIENTIST

BAD HAIR DAY

Franny K. Stein
MAD SCIENTIST

BAD HAIR DAY

JIM BENTON

SIMON & SCHUSTER BOOKS FOR YOUNG READERS

NEW YORK LONDON TORONTO SYDNEY NEW DELHI

SIMON & SCHUSTER BOOKS FOR YOUNG READERS

An imprint of Simon & Schuster Children's Publishing Division

1230 Avenue of the Americas, New York, New York 10020

This book is a work of fiction. Any references to historical events, real people, or real places are used fictitiously. Other names, characters, places, and events are products of the author's imagination, and any resemblance to actual events or places or persons, living or dead, is entirely coincidental.

Copyright © 2019 by Jim Benton

All rights reserved, including the right of reproduction in whole or in part in any form.

SIMON & SCHUSTER BOOKS FOR YOUNG READERS

is a trademark of Simon & Schuster, Inc.

For information about special discounts for bulk purchases, please contact Simon & Schuster Special Sales at 1-866-506-1949 or business@simonandschuster.com.

The Simon & Schuster Speakers Bureau can bring authors to your live event. For more information or to book an event, contact the Simon & Schuster Speakers Bureau at 1-866-248-3049 or visit our website at www.simonspeakers.com.

Also available in a Simon & Schuster Books for Young Readers hardcover edition

Book design by Tom Daly

The text for this book was set in Neue Captain Kidd Lowercase.

The illustrations for this book were rendered in pen, ink, and watercolor.

Manufactured in the United States of America / 0921 OFF

First Simon & Schuster Books for Young Readers paperback edition July 2020

2 4 6 8 10 9 7 5 3

The Library of Congress has cataloged the hardcover edition as follows:

Names: Benton, Jim, author, illustrator.

Title: Bad hair day / Jim Benton.

Description: First edition. | New York : Simon & Schuster Books for Young Readers, [2019] | Series: Franny K. Stein, mad scientist ; [#8] | Summary: Franny tries to follow her mother's suggestion to change her appearance, but by turning hair styling into a science experiment she creates some very greedy pigtails that terrorize the town.

Identifiers: LCCN 2018015661 | ISBN 9781534413375 (hardcover : alk. paper) | ISBN 9781534413382 (pbk) | ISBN 9781534413399 (ebook)

Subjects: | CYAC: Science—Experiments—Fiction. | Hair—Fiction. | Dogs—Fiction. | Mothers and daughters—Fiction. | Humorous stories.

Classification: LCC PZ7.B447547 Bad 2019 | DDC [Fic]—dc23

LC record available at https://lccn.loc.gov/2018015661

For Nava

ACKNOWLEDGMENTS

Editors: Krista Vitola and Catherine Laudone

Designer: Tom Daly

Art Director: Lucy Cummins

Production Editor: Dorothy Gribbin

Production Manager: Chava Wolin

Thanks to Kristin LeClerc

CONTENTS

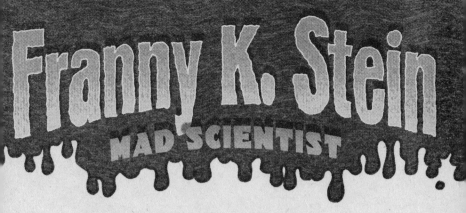

BAD HAIR DAY

CHAPTER ONE

FRANNY'S HOUSE

The Stein family lived in the pretty pink house with the lovely purple shutters down at the end of Daffodil Street. Everything about the house was bright and cheery.

But, of course, the outside of a house is never as interesting as what's going on inside it.

And inside this house, behind the little round upstairs window, something interesting was always going on, because this was the bedroom and laboratory of Franny K. Stein, Mad Scientist.

Last week, for example, Franny developed
a giant sea horse, and the day before that she
worked on a way to fly based on how bats
flap their wings.

Those projects became pretty expensive, so Franny needed to get a piggy bank to save her money in.

Of course, being a mad scientist, she created her piggy bank from a real live pig, which meant that she had to learn all she could about pigs.

This got pretty messy, but she didn't mind getting messy, because that's just what happens when you're doing mad science.

CHAPTER TWO

BEAUTY AND THE BEASTLY

Mad science isn't *just* messy. Mad science isn't always pretty, either.

There's nothing pretty about a hamburger that makes its own ketchup. Especially when you bite into it.

And nobody ever called Franny's Totally Circular Wiener Dog pretty.

The word most people would use is "disturbing."

Still, Mom liked the wiener dog better than when Franny invented a spray-on Halloween costume that made Franny completely break out in giant warts.

"It's so much faster than putting on a costume," Franny explained.

Mom had to admit that it was really fast, but when Franny decided she didn't want to wash the warts off, her mom felt like she had to talk to her about it.

"You know why nobody ever wants to pet Igor, right?" her mom asked her, wiping off her warts.

Igor was Franny's lab assistant. He wasn't a pure Lab. He was also part poodle, part Chihuahua, part beagle, part spaniel, part shepherd, and part some kind of weaselly thing that wasn't even exactly a dog.

"It's because of the way Igor looks," Mom continued.

"What's wrong with how he looks?" Franny asked.

Mom stammered, "Well, he's kind of . . . I mean . . . Igor's not going to win any beauty contests, Franny.

"And wouldn't you like it if he was, you know, a better-looking dog?"

Igor tried to look better looking.

Franny had never noticed anything wrong with Igor's looks.

"Mom, Igor *is* beautiful! He doesn't need to win any contests for me to see that. And look at his adorable puppy-dog eyes." Franny giggled.

Franny held Igor up, and he fluttered his eyelashes at her mom.

"Okay, okay," she said. "Put him down.

"Franny, all I'm trying to say is that maybe you might think it's fun to dress up a little occasionally, or wear your hair different. You might like to be fancy sometimes."

Mom draped a beautiful coat on Franny, and she looked in the mirror.

She started combing Franny's hair and grabbed a can of hair spray.

"You know what hair spray does?" she said as she shook the can.

"It holds hair in place. I know, Mom, I just don't—"

"Okay. We'll skip the hair spray. But how about a blow-dryer: Do you know what this does?" her mom said.

"I'm guessing it does something to your hair?" Franny replied.

"Well, yes, but there's a little more to it than that."

"Thanks, Mom, but it just doesn't feel like me," Franny said, taking off the coat. "I don't think I need to know anything about this stuff."

Mom smiled and hugged Franny.

"Okay, okay. That's perfectly fine. Do what feels right, but know that you can always change your mind. You can explore different options whenever you want," she said, and walked out of Franny's laboratory.

"At least don't spray the warts back on," she called from the hallway.

Franny looked in the mirror.

"Does Mom want *me* to change?" she whispered.

"I wear my special lab suit to protect me from dangerous chemicals. I wear my hair in pigtails so it doesn't get caught in machinery. I never wear nail polish because the pretty colors will just cause some creature in the lab to chew my fingers off.

"Cosmetics, hair stuff, fancy clothes. They aren't for me, Igor. I just don't understand them," Franny said.

Lightning cracked outside.

"Wait a second," Franny said. "Do you hear what I am saying?

"I understand electricity and dynamite and tarantulas and chemistry."

Igor held up a recently modified teddy bear.

"Yes," Franny agreed. "And surgically implanting a brain in a teddy bear. I understand that, too."

The teddy bear smiled.

"But you know, Igor, science is also about exploring the things we *don't* understand.

"It's about reaching higher and exploring the unknown!

"Even if it's the really super-weird stuff that moms like.

"Do you see what I mean? I can't ignore something because I don't understand it. Not understanding things is exactly what attracted me to science in the first place."

Igor nodded.

"Mom's products are super kooky, Igor, but c'mon—we *love* kooky stuff."

Igor tried to smile and nod in agreement, but the truth was, he really didn't like kooky stuff very much.

"Tomorrow we get as weird as Mom!"
Franny yelled triumphantly.

CHAPTER THREE

LET'S FACE IT

Makeup is an interesting thing, Igor. Mom only wears it sometimes, but when she does, it's just the right amount. Look what happens when we put on a little too much."

"Can you imagine if a clown walked out in front of an audience without *enough* makeup on? He would be nothing but lovely, and that would be terrible for a clown.

"That's why I invented this," Franny said, lifting a rather dangerous-looking device. "It's my Cosmetic Bazooka. It's filled with regular old makeup, but it's all carefully measured so that with just one blast you look perfect."

Franny pointed it at Igor and pulled the trigger.

Igor ducked just in time, leaving a perfectly made-up face on the wall behind him.

Franny giggled.

"Oh, Igor, you act like I've never shot you
in the face before."

CHAPTER FOUR

FRANNY NAILS IT

Mom likes her nail polish, too, Igor," Franny said, and began brushing some of her new chemical formula onto her own nails.

"But I was thinking, her fingernails aren't *really* nails at all, are they?"

Franny wiggled her fingers at Igor.

"Watch what *my* nail polish does."

Suddenly long, pointy nails sprang out
from Franny's fingertips, and she slashed
them back and forth in the air.

"Now *these* are something special," she
said, and she plunged them through two
boards, nailing them together.

"I'll bet Mom would like these. Don't you
think so?"

Igor wasn't sure if Franny's mom would like them, but he knew how much he would like to have those the next time he was bullied by the mean cat next door.

Franny broke the nails off with a snap and held the board up for inspection.

"Did you see how fast those grew? And how long?"

Igor looked at the nails. They seemed to wriggle a bit, as though they might actually be ... *alive.*

"I have another idea," Franny said.

CHAPTER FIVE
TEACHING YOUR DOG TO HEEL

You know how Mom wears those high heels sometimes? They're, like, three inches tall. Well, if she likes those, I can make some she's going to *love*."

Franny carefully placed the shoes on her feet.

"I made a few adjustments to the formula, and I changed the nail polish to shoe polish."

She smeared some on the shoes.

In seconds the heels erupted into five-foot-tall spikes.

Franny wobbled as she walked around the room.

"What do you think, Igor? Pretty nice, right?"

Igor scurried around frantically. He didn't want to get stepped on as Franny modeled her shoes.

Just then Franny caught sight of herself in the mirror. She tugged at one of her pig-tails. "You know, Igor, this stuff might work on lots of other things! Maybe I can make *everything* grow."

She jumped out of the shoes and let them fall to the ground. Igor picked one up and examined it. It didn't wiggle like the finger-nails had.

He dropped it and ran after Franny, who was already busy with the next experiment.

CHAPTER SIX

HAIR WE GO

I've made some more adjustments to the formula," Franny told Igor as she handed a little bottle to him.

It bubbled and fizzed, and a little cloud of smoke puffed out the top.

"Put just three drops onto each pigtail," she said. "No more than that."

Igor nodded and carefully dripped the formula onto Franny's hair.

"It tingles," she said.

And her hair started to frizzle. And frazzle. And suddenly, with a strange, creaky whine, it began to grow.

And grow.

It grew until it draped all around her on the floor.

"It worked! It's a success!"

Franny tossed her hair around and around, so much so that it knocked over a beaker. Then it got caught on a table leg.

She tried to get it loose and stumbled into a cage of monsters, knocking the door open and setting them loose in the lab.

"What a mess! I can't get anything done with this hair everywhere. Igor, hand me the scissors, and I'll cut this useless stuff off right this minute."

Before Igor could grab the scissors, one of Franny's pigtails stretched out and grabbed the scissors *by* *itself.*

It handed them gently to Franny.

"Whoa!" she said. "Did you see that, Igor? These pigtails might be pretty good assistants. Maybe I'll keep them around for now."

Igor frowned. *He* was Franny's assistant, and he didn't think she needed any new ones.

"And I wonder," Franny said. "Maybe if we used just a couple more drops . . ."

CHAPTER SEVEN

NOTHING COULD POSSIBLY GO WRONG

Franny moved around the lab, suspended by her pigtails, which walked her around like big, fuzzy legs.

She used them to grab a device on a very high shelf and stretch for a beaker that had rolled under a sea monster's fishbowl.

"Isn't this great, Igor?" She grinned. "I can reach everything!"

Igor pointed at the super-tall shoes.

"Those are great, but shoes aren't alive the way hair is. They can't move on their own."

Igor scowled.

"I know what you're thinking, Igor. This experiment was supposed to be all about Mom stuff, so why would Mom be interested in living pigtails?

"Well, watch this...."

Franny snapped her fingers, and her pigtails sprang into a brand-new hairdo. She snapped again, and they changed into another style. With each snap they became something new.

"Now, you *know* Mom is going to love that," Franny said. "So much faster than fiddling around with her hair spray and brushes and blow-dryers and stuff."

CHAPTER EIGHT

FRANNY'S HAIR LETS HER DOWN

Late that night Igor was awakened by the sound of somebody rattling through cabinets.

And at first he wasn't worried about it—he figured it was probably just the monsters stirring in their cages.

But as his eyes opened slowly, he saw that one of Franny's pigtails had stretched all the way over to the shelf where she kept her formula.

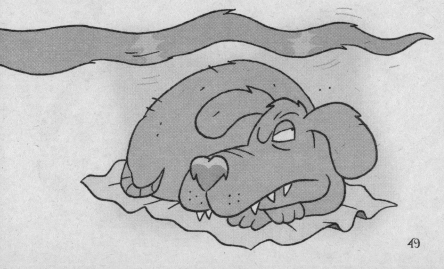

The pigtail was trying to get the bottle open when Igor pounced! He tried as hard as he could to wrestle it from its hairy grasp.

The scuffle woke up Franny, who jumped out of bed to see what was the matter.

"Trying to sneak more of the growth formula?" Franny asked, and she shook her head sadly.

"I'm disappointed in you but not very surprised. I know all about pigs. I learned that pigs are greedy by nature. I guess pigtails are too," she said.

She patted Igor.

"Good job, Igor. I'll do something about these two little piggies in the morning," she said, and walked sleepily back to her bed.

CHAPTER NINE

SHEAR MADNESS

T he next morning Franny shuffled into the bathroom to brush her teeth and wash her face. But when she looked in the mirror, something was different.

"MY HAIR!" she shrieked as she charged out of the bathroom.

"Igor! What happened to my hair?"

Igor didn't answer.

He wasn't in his bed. He wasn't playing in the bathtub. He wasn't watching cartoons on her computer.

Finally she found him tied up by a thick cluster of her own purple hair.

"Those pigtails must have cut themselves off my head!" she shouted. Franny went to examine the bottle of growth formula.

"And I'll bet they doused themselves with more of this stuff."

Franny ran to the window and looked through her telescope.

"I see them! They're in town already," she yelled. "Gosh, they're so fast! I'll never catch them on foot."

She ran downstairs and found Mom watching something on the news.

"Reports are coming in from all over town," Mom said. "From beauty salons and barbershops! Two strange beasts are on a rampage.

"They say they're two large, piglike creatures that are eating everything."

Franny's mom looked at her sternly.

"Franny, you wouldn't know anything about this, would you?" she said.

"Mom, it's two weird creatures on a rampage," Franny said. "Of course I know something about this. Rampaging creatures are kind of my thing.

"They're basically pigs, Mom. Don't worry. All they want to do is get bigger," Franny said. "And they're not eating *everything*. They're made out of hair, and that's all they're after. They're just going to go after people's pets, and when those are gone, they'll start eating the hair on people's heads. Maybe they'll chew the beards off men's faces."

Franny laughed.

"So it's not *everything*."

"That still sounds pretty bad, Franny," Mom said. "Maybe somebody else should handle this," her mom added hopefully. "Maybe these are somebody else's rampaging creatures."

"Oh, they're my pigs, all right, and I'm sure that nobody can stop them but me."

Franny dug through a drawer.

"But I'll need a rubber band."

"You're going to defeat them with a rubber band?" Franny's mom howled.

"There's no time to explain," Franny said fiercely, and she pulled what was left of her hair into a ponytail and quickly twisted a rubber band around it.

CHAPTER TEN

IGOR GETS PUMPED

Franny dribbled a couple drops of her formula onto her ponytail and grabbed her scissors.

Franny's mom watched in amazement as Franny's ponytail turned into a full-size pony.

Franny snipped it off and climbed onto its back, then grabbed her mom's purse as she galloped out the front door.

Igor started to follow her, but she paused and shouted back at him.

"You're too deliciously furry! They'd gobble you up! Stay here with Mom!"

Franny then reared up on her ponytail and galloped out of sight.

As Franny got closer and closer to the pig-tails, she saw the destruction they had left in their path.

On the streets lay dolls without braids, peaches without fuzz, and completely bald caterpillars.

"How much hair can these things eat?" she said.

By the time she caught up to them, they were munching up a wig store.

"Hold it right there, pigs!" Franny shouted. Her pigtails stopped eating and ran toward her and her beautiful pony.

She pulled out her mom's cordless blow-dryer and hit them with its full force.

"I'll bet *this* will make you more manage-able!" she shouted.

But her idea didn't work out as she'd planned.

It just made the pigtails fluffier and puffier. They were even bigger now than before.

"I guess I *don't* know how blow-dryers work," Franny said. "I should have paid more attention to Mom."

Back at home, Igor watched in horror as the pigtails loomed over Franny on TV.

He raced up the stairs, grabbed some things from Franny's lab, and bolted out the door.

Franny frowned at the big, hairy pigtails as they pinned her up against a wall.

"Get behind me, ponytail," she said, trying to protect it from the pigs. "I won't let them get you, too."

One of the pigs snarled and lunged for Franny.

Her ponytail whinnied and jumped in front of her. The pig swallowed it down in one oinky gulp.

"That was one really nice hairdo," Franny said as the second huge pig swelled up and growled at her.

"This looks like the end," Franny said to herself, and she shook her fist at the monster. "Okay, then. Come and get me!"

But just then Franny saw Igor rise up behind the pig.

"Why is he so tall?" she said to herself.

CHAPTER ELEVEN

YOUR HAIR IS
REALLY MESSED UP

Igor wobbled around awkwardly on the high heels. He was trying to sneak up on the pig with a pair of scissors.

Amazing! He must have put more formula on the shoes. That's why he's so tall, Franny thought.

But what's even more amazing, Franny said to herself, *is that a dog in a pair of thirty-foot heels thinks he can sneak up on anybody.*

The pigtail spun around and, with a single snap, plucked Igor right out of the shoes and swallowed him whole.

"NOOOO!" Franny cried. "IGOR!!!"

The distraction gave Franny just enough time to hide behind a trash can.

"Igor did that to save me," Franny whispered, her eyes welling up with tears. "He would have done anything for me. He would have done anything for anybody."

She watched as the pigtails sniffed the air and began shambling down the street.

"They want more hair," she whispered. "No more Miss Nice Girl. These pigs need to be stopped! And I bet I know where they're headed. . . .

"The zoo!"

CHAPTER TWELVE

WE'RE IN PIG TROUBLE NOW

Franny chased after the pigtails.

"I have no idea how I'm going to stop these things," she said. "I have to think!"

The pigtails crashed through the front gates of the zoo and walked right past the alligators and tortoises.

"They don't have fur, so the pigs aren't interested in them," Franny said.

She watched as the pigs stopped to read a sign. One of them licked his lips as he did.

"Not the orangutans!" Franny whispered as the pigs waddled off toward the apes.

In desperation, Franny rushed up and grabbed a handful of one of the pigtails. She yanked it as hard as she could.

"Nobody likes to have their hair pulled!"

ORANGUTANS

With one mighty swat, the pigtail knocked Franny aside.

Franny sat up and groaned.

"I've really messed up this time."

And then she heard scissors snipping.

And snipping.

And snipping.

Fanny stood up and stared as she saw a little pink paw holding scissors and snipping its way out of the back of one of the pigtails.

It was Igor!

He had snipped his way out.

And so that the pigtails wouldn't want to swallow him again, he had also snipped off all his hair while he was in there.

He stood there and held the scissors proudly. He looked triumphant, pink, and naked.

One of the pigtails turned around and looked at him.

"Ew," it said, and kept walking toward the orangutans.

Franny ran up and hugged him.

"Don't listen to that pig," she said. "You're beautiful."

Igor handed her the scissors and pointed at the pigtails.

"I can't do much with these," she said. "They're too little. But you're right. We have to do something. After they eat the orangutans, they'll go for the buffaloes and the bears."

Igor handed her the backpack of things he'd brought from the lab. Franny dug through it.

"I think I have an idea," she said.

Chapter Thirteen
SPLIT ENDS

The pigs climbed over the fence and into the orangutan enclosure. The orangutans cowered and squealed in fear.

One of the pigs reached out a big, hairy hoof, grabbed the tiniest orangutan, and lifted it up to its mouth.

"This has to work, Igor," Franny said. "We don't have much of this left."

She pulled a mascara bottle from the backpack, dipped the tiny brush in the formula, and carefully applied it to Igor's eyelashes.

Long, lush lashes erupted from his eye-lids.

"Now let's see those beautiful puppy-dog eyes," Franny said, and giggled.

SPROING!

Igor began flapping his lashes, and Franny hopped onto his back.

The two rose into the sky, lifted by Igor's masterful fluttering.

"Head for those pigs," Franny growled.

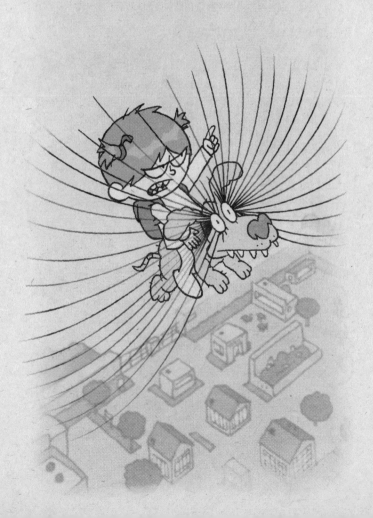

They swooped over and grabbed the orangutan just before the pig could swallow it.

"Surrender now," Franny said, "or be glamorized."

The pigs hissed at her as Igor flew around and came at them fast.

The pigtails lunged and twisted, trying to grab Franny and Igor as they zigzagged around, weaving in and out, until...

the pigtails fell over on the ground, wriggling and snorting, and gorgeously braided.

Igor dived down to the ground as Franny shook a hair spray can.

As soon as they got close enough, Franny blasted the pigs with a cloud of hair spray, holding them in that position, unable to move.

Igor landed next to them, and Franny stuck her finger in the bottle of formula.

"I'll bet there's just enough left...."

She pulled out her finger, and a giant, sharp nail sprang from the end of it.

"This won't hurt a bit, pigs," she said, and she cut away strands of hair until her ponytail wriggled out and snuggled her thankfully.

"Let's go home. I have a little work to do in the lab."

CHAPTER FOURTEEN

THE TAIL COMES TO AN END

Franny's mom walked into Franny's laboratory.

"Nice work on those pigtail things," she said.

"Thanks, Mom."

"Of course, you probably shouldn't have created them in the first place."

Franny laughed.

"You're right, Mom. But things like that happen to people all the time." Franny shrugged.

"They don't, Franny. Things like that don't happen to people all the time. Things like that only happen to you."

Franny showed her mom a jar with her old pigtails in it.

"Look. I washed the formula out of some of the leftover hair and constructed brand-new pigtails for myself. They're perfectly normal now. I'm going to reattach them."

Franny put her pigtails back into place and shook her head to make sure they were stuck.

"What happened to your ponytail?" Mom asked.

"It wanted to go back to the zoo. I think it fell in love with that baby orangutan."

Franny's mom smiled.

"Oh! And I have a surprise for you!" Franny said, and she ran to get something from the closet.

She handed her mom a purple fur coat.

"I used some of the giant pigtails and I made you a fur coat. You can change the style, too, just by snapping your fingers!"

"This isn't going to try to eat anybody, is it?"

"Nope. The pigtails were greedy because they were pigs. The greed was the problem, not the hair.

"But I got rid of the greediness. Now they're delighted to just make somebody happy by being a coat."

Franny's mom tried on the coat.

"It's lovely! But how did you get rid of the greed?" she asked.

"I added a dash of Igor's fur. He's the least selfish creature in the whole world. The greed just went away."

Franny's mom looked at the ground. She
felt a little ashamed.

"You were right about Igor all along,
Franny. I wasn't looking at him in the right
way. He *is* beautiful. Maybe the most beautiful dog that ever lived."

Franny's mom looked around.

"Hey, where is Igor, anyway?"

"I sent him to the store to pick up a few things. I was thinking of trying that new shampoo you suggested. He won't be long."

"The store? But I thought he was afraid of walking past that mean cat next door."

"I don't think that's going to be a problem anymore," Franny said.

Jim Benton

is a *New York Times* bestselling writer and cartoonist whose unique brand of humor has been seen on toys, television, T-shirts, greeting cards, and even underwear. Franny K. Stein is the first character he's created especially for young children. A husband and father of two, he lives in Michigan, where he works in a studio that really and truly does have creepy stuff in it.

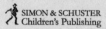